NICK
SpongeBob SquarePants

Oh, Barnacles!

SpongeBob's Handbook for Bad Days

by David Lewman

Simon Spotlight/Nickelodeon
New York   London   Toronto   Sydney

Stephen Hillenburg

Based on the TV series *SpongeBob SquarePants*® created by Stephen Hillenburg as seen on Nickelodeon®

SIMON SPOTLIGHT
An imprint of Simon & Schuster Children's Publishing Division
1230 Avenue of the Americas, New York, New York 10020
Copyright © 2005 Viacom International Inc. All rights reserved.
NICKELODEON, *SpongeBob SquarePants*, and all related titles, logos, and characters are registered trademarks of Viacom International Inc.
All rights reserved, including the right of reproduction in whole or in part in any form.
SIMON SPOTLIGHT and colophon are registered trademarks of Simon & Schuster, Inc.
Manufactured in the United States of America
First Edition
2 4 6 8 10 9 7 5 3
ISBN-13: 978-1-4169-0641-4
ISBN-10: 1-4169-0641-X

Table of Contents

How to Use This Handbook,
by SpongeBob

I'M READY! To tell you how to use this book, that is. Are YOU ready? Great!

Here's how you do it. Find a good friend, like Squidward. Then one of you can read what's written under each of the blanks. (Like "noun," "verb," or "something smelly.") The other person can think of words to go in those blanks. Once you've come up with words for all the blanks, you can read the whole thing out loud. And LAUGH!

When the blank calls for a NOUN, think of a thing, a place, or even a person. Pineapple, Bikini Bottom, and squirrel are all examples of nouns.

When the blank calls for a VERB, think of an action word—a word about doing something. Fry, sleep, and giggle are all examples of verbs.

Sometimes the blank will need an "-ing verb." That just means a verb with an "-ing" on the end, like frying, sleeping, and giggling.

Sometimes the blank will need a "past-tense verb." Fried, slept, and giggled are examples of past-tense verbs.

Some of the blanks need an ADJECTIVE. An adjective is a word that describes what something is like. Wet, yellow, and porous are all adjectives. (They're also very good things to be!)

Some blanks need ADVERBS. An adverb is a word that describes how something is done. It usually ends in "ly." Enthusiastically, slowly, and stupidly are adverbs.

Sometimes the blank will ask you to think of something specific, like "type of food," "body part," or "something disgusting." Just come up with whatever the blank asks for.

Now you know how to use this book. **YOU'RE READY!!!**

How to Survive a Jellyfish Attack, by SpongeBob

Everyone knows that jellyfish are usually as _____ as
                                              adjective
a(n) _____. But when they attack, they can be as
      noun

_____ as a(n) _____ full of _____s. If you
 adjective   type of container   type of animal
_____ quickly, you won't get _____.
  verb   adjective

The first thing you should do is cover your _____ with
                                              body part
a(n) _____, so the jellyfish will think you're
       noun
a(n) _____.
      noun

Next you've got to _____ as fast as you can. While
                      verb
doing it, yell "Help! Jellyfish are _____ me! Somebody
                                     -ing verb
call a(n) _____!"
          type of worker

If nobody comes to help, try speaking _____ to the
                                        adverb
jellyfish. You might say "Excuse me, but why are you

_____ me? Why don't you go _____
 -ing verb   verb
_____?"
name of someone you know

And if all else fails, try jumping in a pool of _____.
                                                  gross liquid
Jellyfish really hate _____. I think.
                      same gross liquid

6

HOW TO AVOID BEING ATTACKED
BY JELLYFISH

🪼 Never _____ into a jellyfish hive.
      verb

🪼 Never steal their jelly to smear on _____.
                                    type of food

🪼 Don't _____ in Jellyfish Fields, singing, "I'm a big
          verb

_____ who needs to be attacked."
noun

7

How to Survive Living Under a Rock, by Patrick

Living under a rock is really _____. It's a great place
to _____, to _____, and even to _____. But it's
     verb   verb
important to keep some simple _____s in mind.
                               noun

First choose a rock that isn't too _____. Go
                               adjective
underneath it, and see if you can _____ comfortably.
                             verb

Once you've chosen a rock to live under, master the
fine art of _____. This is really _____
           ing verb   adjective
if you're going to live under a rock.

Once every _____
number
weeks, _____ the
verb
rock. If you don't, it's

liable to get all

_____ and to smell
adjective
like _____.
gross food

Most important of all, never ever _____ under
verb
your rock. If you're going to do that, you'd be better off living

under a(n) _____.
noun

How to Survive a Boring Job, by Squidward

My job at the Krusty Krab is about as exciting as watching _____ drip
<small>kind of liquid</small>
into a(n) _____, so I know what
<small>type of container</small>
I'm talking about.

Always try to arrive at least

_____ hours late. Sure, your boss
<small>number</small>
may punish you by making you clean the

_____ with a(n) _____,
<small>noun</small>   <small>noun</small>
but you'll suffer a little less boredom.

Whenever possible, close your

_____s and imagine
<small>body parts</small>
you're playing music

with a(n) _____
<small>noun</small>
or dancing the lead role

in "_____ Lake."
<small>animal</small>
Play fun tricks on your

fellow employees, like putting

_____ in their hats.
<small>food you hate</small>
Or telling them it's

"Wear-a(n)-_____-to-Work-Day."
<small>ocean creature</small>

Stare at the ceiling, searching for _____ shapes.
adjective

Once I saw a stain that looked like_____
name of a person you know

eating _____ dipped in _____.
your favorite candy   _disgusting substance_

Try to leave at least _____ hours early.
number

But the best way to survive a boring job is to never

_____ one in the first place. On second thought take
verb

mine before I lose my _____!
body part

How to Tell if Your Job Is Boring

Every time you _____ at work you
verb

_____ fall asleep.
adverb

Counting the _____s is the most exciting
noun

part of your day.

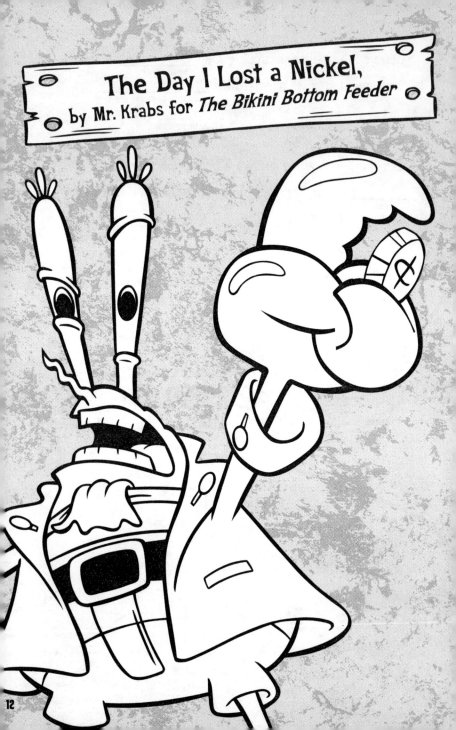

The Day I Lost a Nickel,
by Mr. Krabs for *The Bikini Bottom Feeder*

I've read all the stories you've run in this _____ newspaper about
adjective

people's bad days. But those are nothing compared to the _____ day I
adjective

_____ lost my nickel.
adverb

It was early in the morning, and I was just _____ along, minding my own _____.
ing verb   noun

As usual I was carrying my favorite nickel in my _____.
type of container

All of a sudden I stepped on a(n) _____ and fell
noun

flat on my _____. Then I heard a sound that made my
body part

_____ _____. It was my _____ nickel rolling
body part verb   adjective

away!

I jumped up and ran after it faster than a(n) _____
animal

being chased by a(n) _____. But I just wasn't
animal

_____ enough.
adjective

My nickel _____ into a hole and _____. It was
past tense verb   past tense verb

so _____ I _____ like a baby.
adjective   past tense verb

Luckily I earned another nickel only _____ minutes
number

later. I love that nickel as if it were my own _____!
noun

13

How to Deal with a Sarcastic Parrot, by Patchy the Pirate

My parrot, Potty, is even more sarcastic than _____.
_{person you know}
But since I've had Potty for _____ years, I know how to
_{number}
deal with a sarcastic parrot. When it comes to sarcastic

_____s, you're on your own.
_{animal}

Don't try _____ asking the parrot to stop being sarcastic.
_{adverb}
That'll work about as well as asking the Flying Dutchman to fill

your _____s with _____ .
_{article of clothing}   _{your favorite kind of meat}

And if you threaten to punish the parrot, it'll fly away faster

than you can say "_____." Plus it might grab your
_{a teacher's name}

_____ with its claws, and that really _____s.
_{body part}   _{verb}

You could try bribing the parrot with _____,
_{type of food}

_____, and a(n) _____. But that'll go over like
_{type of dessert}   _{your favorite toy}

a(n) _____ boat made out of _____
_{adjective}   _{heavy material}

sailing the _____ Sea.
_{sandwich ingredient}

I guess what I'm saying is, if you've

got a parrot that's _____
_{adverb}

sarcastic, you're stuck with a

sarcastic parrot.

How to Defend Yourself Against a Karate Maniac, by <u>Sandy</u>

In Texas, my home state, you rarely _____ any karate

verb

maniacs. But under the sea there must be _____ of

number

them. They jump out and _____ me almost every day!

verb

Especially if I'm anywhere near SpongeBob's house.

The best way to protect yourself is to always wear

a(n) _____ on your head, wrap your body with

noun

_____, and stick your feet in _____s.

material   type of container

If a karate maniac leaps out at you, crouch like a(n) _____
                                                          animal
ready to _____. Your _____ should be tucked, and
           verb   body part
your _____ should be lower than your _____.
      body part   body part
Scream "Get away from me, you _____ _____!"
                               adjective   noun
Try to block the karate chops with your _____.
                                         body part
If you start feeling _____, just call out "Sandy!" I'll
                      adjective
come a-runnin' to _____ that maniac Texas-style!
                   verb

PLACES TO AVOID IF YOU'RE AFRAID OF KARATE MANIACS

❀ Stay at least _____ feet away from SpongeBob's house.
                 number

❀ If you see a pineapple house, _____ immediately.
                                 verb

❀ The Krusty Krab is pretty _____ too.
                            adjective

❀ Actually you should probably _____ away from
                               verb
my _____ tree house, too. I love karate even
   adjective
more than I love _____!
                 your favorite food

The Day My TV Broke,
by Patrick for *The Bikini Bottom Feeder*

THE Bikini Bottom FEEDER

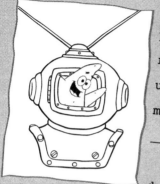

Hello! I know you think you've had days that were really _____ . But wait
adjective
until you hear about the day my _____ TV broke. It was
adjective
_____ !
adjective
It _____ out like any other
past tense verb
day. I woke up, reached for my remote, and _____ turned on my _____ TV. But
adverb   _adjective_
instead of turning on, it just _____ !
past tense verb

I tried to fix it by throwing a(n) _____ at it. But
noun
I missed and hit my _____ instead. Then I picked up
noun
a(n) _____ and _____ TV with it. That just made it
noun   _past tense verb_
_____ .
adjective

So I picked up the TV, climbed up on my _____ , and
piece of furniture
dropped it. Then I tried jumping on it, but I landed on
my _____ instead.
your favorite toy

Then I noticed that instead of using my remote, I'd
tried to turn my TV on with a(n) _____ . Plus it
noun
wasn't plugged in.

What a(n) _____ day!
adjective

19

How to Deal with Bad Guys,
by Mermaidman

I've been dealing with bad guys since I was _____ years
                                               number
old. A lot of people don't _____ this, but the Dirty Bubble and
                            verb
I were in school together. Once he dumped a whole can of

_____ on my head.
type of food
So, to fight EVILdoers, first, put on your _____ costume.
                                            adjective
Otherwise the bad guys will think you're just a regular

_____.
   noun
Next make sure your sidekick is _____ by your side.
                                 -ing verb
I never tackle bad guys without Barnacleboy because he always

remembers to bring the _____s.
                         noun
Don't try _____ the bad guys into being _____
           -ing verb   adjective
because it doesn't work. I've tried, but bad guys are _____
                                                        adverb
EVIL!

Instead set your utility belt to "_____." Press the button,
                                    verb
and start _____. If you don't have a utility belt, try using
           -ing verb
a(n) _____ belt.
      noun
This should handle the bad guys _____, unless they're
                                    adverb
too _____. If they keep on
     adjective
_____, I suggest calling
 -ing verb
Sandy Cheeks for help. She's really

_____.
  adjective
And if one of the bad guys turns out to

be the Dirty Bubble, please dump a can of

_____ on his head for me.
type of food

How to Save Someone at the Beach,
by Larry the Lobster

If you see someone in trouble at the beach, _____ a
_____ verb
lifeguard. (Most lifeguards are _____ and _____,
_____ adjective _____ adjective
like me!)

Next scream "Hey! That guy is _____!" The lifeguard
_____ -ing verb
will _____ off his/her chair and _____ into
_____ verb _____ verb
the water. Next he'll/she'll grab the person by the
_____ and pull him/her out of the water.
_____ body part
The lifeguard will ask if the person feels _____.
_____ adjective
If he/she gets no answer, the lifeguard will use his/her

_____s to pump the water out of the person's
_____ body part
_____. Holding the person's mouth open
_____ body part
with a(n) _____ can be
_____ noun
very helpful!

Once the person seems okay,

you can offer to get

him/her some

_____ and
_____ snack item
_____. This
_____ beverage
will make him/her

feel _____.
_____ adjective

Oh—and if SpongeBob and Patrick try to help, make sure the lifeguard tells them to step _____. Those guys are total
adverb

_____s.
noun

Be Aware: TOP SIGNS a SWiMMeR IS iN TRouBLe

🏐 The swimmer pops out of the water and waves his or her _____s.
body part

🏐 The swimmer yells, "Help! I can't _____!"
verb

🏐 Everyone in the water points to the same person and screams, "Hey, this person can't _____!"
verb

The Day I Met SpongeBob,
by Squidward for *The Bikini Bottom Feeder*

THE Bikini Bottom FEEDER

25¢

Every day of my life is pretty
_____. But I believe the worst
  adjective
day of my life was the day I met
SpongeBob.

It started out like most days. I got
up, took a(n) _____, ate some _____, and started
                noun   *weird food*
playing "You Are the _____ of My Life" on my
                       noun
clarinet. Then I noticed a house going up next door.
The house wasn't a(n) _____ giant head—it was
                        adjective
a pineapple! Workmen were _____ and _____ the
                            ing verb   *ing verb*
pineapple, which I thought was hideous.

Eventually the owner showed up—it was SpongeBob!
Before he even _____ in his own pineapple, he came
                pasttense verb
over to _____ me.
         verb

"Hi!" he said, grinning like a(n) _____. "I'm
                                   noun
SpongeBob—your _____ neighbor—and I know we're
                adjective
going to be friends!"

Since then SpongeBob has been driving me _____! He
                                          adjective
and Patrick are always playing stupid, noisy games like
"Pin the _____ on the _____" or "Who Can
          sea creature   *body part*
Make the Loudest _____" or "Hide-and-Go _____."
                  funny sound   *verb*
So if a pineapple house is built next to yours,
_____! You'll be _____ you did.
 verb   *adjective*

25

How to Survive Being a Sidekick, by Barnacleboy

You may think it's _____ being a sidekick, but believe
                    adjective
me—it's no _____ in the park.
              noun
The superhero you're assigned to can get you into all kinds of

_____(s). If you don't watch out for yourself, you could very
  noun
easily be _____.
          past-tense verb
One of the first things you should do is pick a good name, like

Super _____. Otherwise you might get stuck with
       name
a(n) _____ name like Barnacleboy, which has been _____
     adjective   adverb
driving me nuts for years.

You should also make it clear that you want to be equal partners

with your superhero, so he doesn't treat you like a(n) _____.
                                                         noun
Though you should also make it clear that whenever there's a

dangerous situation, like a(n) _____ _____ or
                               -ing verb   noun
a(n) _____ _____, he should go in first, not you.
     adjective   noun
Oh, and be sure you agree who has to wash the

super_____ every week. You don't want
     noun
to get stuck doing all the _____ work.
                           adjective
And finally try to pick out a costume that

isn't too _____. I mean, look at me—it's
          adjective
embarrassing _____ around in my underpants
             -ing verb
all the time.

26

How to Survive Teaching an Annoying Student, by Mrs. Puff

When I became a teacher I never thought I'd have a student as _____ as

adjective

SpongeBob. Sometimes at the end of a school day I just want to _____ into my

verb

bathtub and _____.

verb

An annoying student will raise his hand at least _____
plural number
times a day. But you should only call on him _____
plural number
times a day.

When your annoying student starts to _____, try
verb
thinking about a nice, peaceful place, like _____ or
location
a place where you can buy lots of chocolate _____s.
noun

Put your annoying student in a group to work on
a(n) _____. Suggest the group go _____ outside,
noun _verb_
for at least _____ hours.
plural number

Do not let your annoying student bring his _____ friend
adjective
to class, especially if his/her name is _____.
name of someone you know
They'll spend the whole day _____.
-ing verb

And no matter how _____ your _____ student
adverb _adjective_
begs to be Hall Monitor, DO NOT ALLOW IT!

Be AWARe: HOW to SPOt an ANNOYiNG StUDeNt

In my experience he'll always have a yellow _____.
body part

His head will be perfectly _____.
shape

And when he laughs, he'll sound like a(n) _____
animal

_____ very _____
-ing verb _adverb_

29

How to Get Rid of a Lousy Crew, by the Flying Dutchman

In all the years I've been haunting the _____ Seas,
<small>number</small>
I've never had a crew worse than SpongeBob and Patrick.

Luckily I know how to get rid of

a(n) _____ crew.
<small>adjective</small>

First try just telling the crew to _____ leave. If your
adverb
ship is _____ enough, that may work.
adjective
If they refuse to leave, I suggest you try _____ like
ing verb
a(n) _____. At night hide their _____s.
animal   noun
Sneak away from your ship and draw a big _____ in
letter of the alphabet
the sand. Then tell your crew that _____'s treasure
name of someone you know
is buried there. While they're digging, sneak back to

your ship and _____.
verb
If all else fails, grab a big

_____ and _____
noun   verb
each crew member over the

head until they all leave.

BE AWARE: HOW TO TELL IF YOUR CREW IS LOUSY

- When you ask for a rope, they hand you a(n) _____.
noun

- They think the poop deck is where you go to _____.
verb

- They keep thinking the sails are ghosts, so every time
they see one, they _____.
verb

31

The Day I Couldn't Find Any Danger,
by Sandy for *The Bikini Bottom Feeder*

THE Bikini Bottom FEEDER

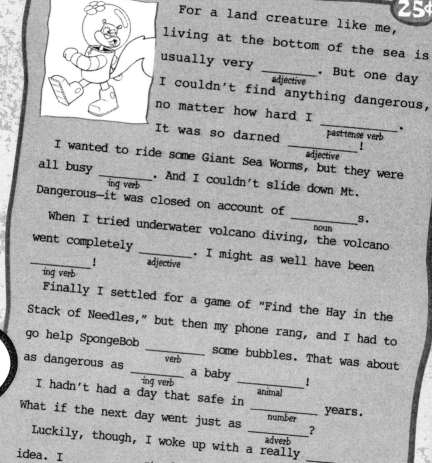

For a land creature like me, living at the bottom of the sea is usually very _____. But one day
adjective
I couldn't find anything dangerous, no matter how hard I _____.
pasttense verb
It was so darned _____!
adjective

I wanted to ride some Giant Sea Worms, but they were all busy _____. And I couldn't slide down Mt.
ing verb
Dangerous—it was closed on account of _____s.
noun

When I tried underwater volcano diving, the volcano went completely _____. I might as well have been
adjective
_____!
ing verb

Finally I settled for a game of "Find the Hay in the Stack of Needles," but then my phone rang, and I had to go help SpongeBob _____ some bubbles. That was about
verb
as dangerous as _____ a baby _____!
ing verb *animal*

I hadn't had a day that safe in _____ years.
number
What if the next day went just as _____?
adverb

Luckily, though, I woke up with a really _____
adjective
idea. I _____ straight to Plankton's restaurant,
pasttense verb
the Chum Bucket, and ordered the breakfast special.
Now that's as dangerous as jumping off a(n) _____
noun
without a(n) _____!
noun *adjective*

How to Survive a Bad Prom Date,
by Pearl

The only thing worse than having a bad date for the prom is waking up with a big _____ on your face. Skin problems
_{noun}

aside, there are ways to survive, no matter how _____ he is.
_{adjective}

Inform your date that you'll be spending at least _____
_{number}

minutes of the prom _____ with your
_{-ing word}

friends.

If your bad date tags along, ask him to get

you some _____ punch. And some
_{type of fruit}

_____s. And maybe some of those
_{your favorite dessert}

_____s, which they only sell in
_{food item}

_____.
_{foreign country}

When he asks you to dance,

say you accidentally dropped a

thousand-pound _____ on
_{noun}

your foot. If he catches you dancing

with someone else, pretend you're your own

twin sister, _____.
_{name of a girl you know}

When it's time for prom-date

photos, tell him he looks cute

with a(n) _____ over his head.
_{container}

34

Always remember that no matter how _____ your adjective
prom date is, he's better than nothing!

Be aware: How to spot a bad prom Date

✿ He drives up to your house in a(n) _____. type of vehicle

✿ He's wearing _____ _____ s and
  color   clothing item
  _____ _____ s.
  color   clothing item

✿ He pins a(n) _____ on your dress.
  noun

✿ The only dance he knows is called "The _____ -ing verb
  _____."
  animal

Arrr, I've been stuck in the same painting for

_____ years. When I first got tossed in here
　　number

_____s were a brand-new invention. But I've survived
　noun

_____, and here are some tips.
　　adverb

Pick a comfortable position to be in. Don't rest your

_____ on your _____, or twist your
body part   body part

_____ until it looks like a(n) _____ .
body part   food item

Get a(n) _____ or some other pet to keep you
       animal

company. My parrot is very _____, and loves
                 adjective

to play _____, although he cheats even
   your favorite game

more than _____.
     name of someone you know

When you're feeling bored, sing a song _____.
                               adverb
Personally my favorite song is "Oh, Who Lives in

a(n) _____ Under the _____."
    food item   something you find in nature

Stay positive: Instead of being stuck in a(n) _____
                                         adjective
painting, you could be stuck in a dartboard.

If anyone asks why you're stuck in a(n) _____
                                     adjective
painting, tell 'em you were framed!

How to Treat a Hole in Your Wallet, by Mr. Krabs

Oh, it's a terrible thing to find a(n) _____ hole in
adjective

your wallet! It's worse than finding a(n) _____
adjective

_____ in your _____s!
animal   _article of clothing_

The most _____ thing to do when you discover the
adjective

hole is check to see if any money is missing. If so, you've got to

find it _____!
adverb

Next take the remaining money out and put

it somewhere safe, like in a metal _____.
kind of container

Make sure you use a strong lock made out of

_____.
kind of material

Then _____ the hole _____ with
verb   _adverb_

a(n) _____. It
noun

should be good and

_____. If you
adjective

_____ the hole
verb

properly, then nothing

should come out when

you put _____ in
noun

your wallet.

Now, you don't want the hole in your wallet to start

_____. So you should let the wallet rest for a few days
   ing verb
in a nice, comfy _____. Be sure to feed your wallet
                        noun
every _____ hours, starting with pennies and working up
       number
to dollars until it can _____ on its own.
                         verb
   Soon your _____ wallet will be as _____ as new!
              adjective   *adjective*

≡BIKINI BOTTOM≡
DRIVER'S LICENSE
A5265661

MR. KRABS

The Day the Krusty Krab Opened, by Plankton for *The Bikini Bottom Feeder*

THE Bikini Bottom FEEDER

I remember that horrible day like it was
_____ . And I'll never _____ it as long as
  noun   verb
I live.

  I had a(n) _____ restaurant called The Chum
           adjective
Bucket, full of _____ customers. Our specialties were
          adjective
fried _____ and baked _____ .
    something gross   something gross

  One day I noticed that a(n) _____ new restaurant had opened
                     adjective
right across the _____ ! It was called The Krusty Krab.
         noun

The minute my customers saw The Krusty Krab they started
_____ . I couldn't stop them no matter how hard I
ing verb
_____ . I saw one customer over at The Krusty Krab
past tense verb
shoving so many _____ s in his mouth, I thought he was
          noun
going to _____ .
     verb

  My _____ customers were all _____ ! I vowed
    adjective   adjective
to get them back, even if I had to _____ _____ s.
                     verb   noun
It was that day that I started trying to steal the recipe
for the _____ Krabby Patty.
    adjective

  So far I've only tried _____
                 number
schemes to steal the recipe. Luckily I've
got at least _____ more. Someday I
       number
will _____ The Krusty Krab!
   verb

P.S. Come into The Chum Bucket for half
off on every third order of fried
_____ .
something gross

CHUM
BUCKET

41

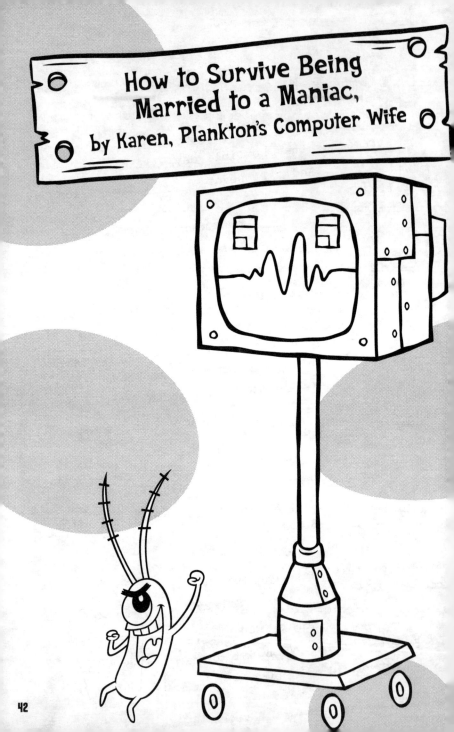

How to Survive Being Married to a Maniac, by Karen, Plankton's Computer Wife

42

Being married to a maniac is about as much fun as _____
                                                          -ing verb
_____s on your head and jumping in a box of _____s.
      noun   noun
But if I can do it for _____ years, so can you.
                        number
    My friend _____ the Robot says, "Always keep
                pet's name
a(n) _____ handy and be ready to _____." (She was
        noun   verb
wrong, but I still send her a box of _____ every year.)
                                        type of food
    Try going along with his plan. If you don't, he may _____
                                                             verb
you with a(n) _____.
                 noun
    Offer him a warm bowl of _____s and a glass of
                                  noun
_____ to distract him from all that evil talk.
type of liquid
    Suggest he get a new job, like _____ for _____s
                                      -ing verb   noun
or play a sport, like _____ ball, which will help him
                        type of fruit
burn off _____s.
            noun
    Buy him a copy of How to Stop Being a Maniac, by

_____ _____. The chapter on _____
friend's first name   vegetable   -ing verb
your evil laugh is really _____.
                             adjective
    If none of this works, shut down for _____ hours—
                                            number
unless you're not a computer. Then you'll just have to

_____.
   verb

Face it: I'm a(n) _____ genius. I went to college at
                        adjective
_____ University. I got really good grades, except in
pet's name
_____, _____, and _____. So I've figured
school subject   *school subject*   *a sport*
out more than _____ ways to attempt to steal a recipe.
                 number

The first thing to do is decide which recipe you want to steal.

Is it for stewed _____s with _____ sauce?
                   vegetable   *ice-cream flavor*
_____ fricassee? _____ loaf with extra _____
kind of meat   *food item*   *adjective*
crumbles on top?

Next find out who has the _____ recipe. You could
                              adjective
either look it up on the _____ or just walk around town
                              noun
_____.
-ing verb

Then you've got to find out where the recipe is _____.
                                                      past tense verb
It might be under a(n) _____. Or in a(n) _____.
                          noun   *noun*
Or even locked away in someone's _____ _____.
                                     adjective   *noun*

Finally you've got to steal that recipe, and you've got to do it
_____. Once you've got the _____ recipe, please
adverb   *adjective*
tell me how you did it. Maybe I can use your _____
                                                 adjective
method to _____ get my _____s on the Krabby
              adverb   *body part*
Patty recipe!

The Day I Lost Gary,
by SpongeBob for *The Bikini Bottom Feeder*

THE Bikini Bottom FEEDER

25¢

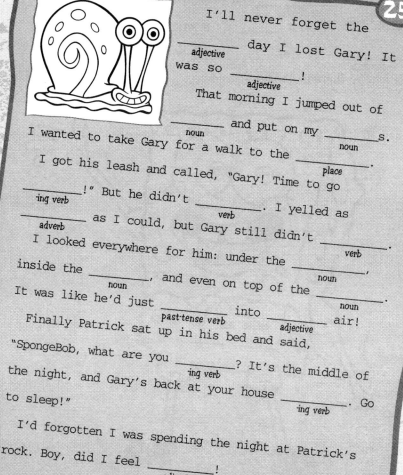

I'll never forget the

_____ day I lost Gary! It
_{adjective}
was so _____!
_{adjective}

That morning I jumped out of

_____ and put on my _____s.
_{noun} _{noun}

I wanted to take Gary for a walk to the _____.
_{place}

I got his leash and called, "Gary! Time to go

_____!" But he didn't _____. I yelled as
_{ing verb} _{verb}

_____ as I could, but Gary still didn't _____.
_{adverb} _{verb}

I looked everywhere for him: under the _____,
_{noun}

inside the _____, and even on top of the _____.
_{noun} _{noun}

It was like he'd just _____ into _____ air!
_{past-tense verb} _{adjective}

Finally Patrick sat up in his bed and said,

"SpongeBob, what are you _____? It's the middle of
_{ing verb}

the night, and Gary's back at your house _____. Go
_{ing verb}

to sleep!"

I'd forgotten I was spending the night at Patrick's
rock. Boy, did I feel _____!
_{adjective}

47

Good-bye, Thanks, and the End

Thanks, _____, for helping to fill up this _____
         your name   *adjective*
book! Without your _____ it would have been completely
                        noun
_____, like a(n) _____ without a(n) _____!
adjective   *animal*   *noun*
I hope this brings you and your _____s a lot of laughs!
                                    noun

THE _____ END
           adjective